Fairy Tales

by:

A.F. Earnest

A.F. Earnest

ISBN: 9781549936326

This story is a work of fiction. Maybe.

Social Media:
Twitter: https://twitter.com/Mikasacus

Table of Contents

A.F. Earnest

Act One

A.F. Earnest

The Bird

A sharp breath cut through the musty air, followed by the coughs and sputters of a neglected vocal tract. It hadn't been used in a week. At least a week, maybe more, maybe less. It had experienced enough weeks without talking to know what a week could feel like, even without a clock.

A man, the owner of the previously mentioned vocal tract, lifted his arched body from his bed. He kicked his legs to the floor, stirring up a cloud of thick dust that floated around the empty room.

He was alone. The only furniture in his little room was the bed he found himself sitting on. There was a window in front of him and a towering metallic door to his left, with a small button below an intercom, and a slit at the threshold.

The man's eyes met the window. He chuckled. Mrs. Gratis was looking beautiful this morning. He could tell it was morning just like he could tell how long a week lasts without a clock.

A feint sliver of light seeped through the window and found itself on his lap.

In a manic burst, the man threw himself from the bed and hurried to the window.

"Good morning, Mrs. Gratis, how are you this morning?" he asked. His spindly finger brushed gently across the windowsill. The man flicked the newly collected dust on his fingertip to the floor in disgust. His face recoiled, as though he had just touched a rotting corpse.

The man leaned forward, being very careful not to make contact with the ray of light coming from the window. He risked a peek outside.

Clouds. Clouds and blue. There was another sill outside, tucked under the windowpane.

"Ah, Mr. Ensom, I see Mrs. Gratis still has you separated by a glass wall, eh? I know how it can be. With women that is," chuckled the man. The windowsill struggled to reply.

Without warning, a blur flashed into view. The man flinched. He fell to the cold concrete floor with a gasp. He got onto his knees. Frozen, quivering, his hands clenched his head. Slowly, like an animal, he crawled back to the window above, digging his gnawed nails into the cement wall to lift himself. He forced his eyes to the source of the disturbance. There was a bird sitting on Mr. Ensom, the windowsill.

He put his face against the window and eyed the bird. It was, as far as he could remember, a swallow. Beautiful little thing, shimmery blue feathers with an orange neck. The man and the swallow stared at each other until the man felt like a week had passed. He thought to himself how good he was at telling time with nothing but his instincts. Even without a clock.

A.F. Earnest

The man strained. He felt something. Something familiar. He only felt this way when the nurses would come through the metal door and stand in his room. A simple look, a needle in the arm, he couldn't tell. They would come in and he would feel. He was feeling it again. Right now.

"Hello," chirped the bird on the other side of the window. The man held his breath and turned his head to the door. He felt as if it were coming closer. As if the walls were compressing and pushing out his air. He turned back to the bird.

"Yes, hello, you're standing on my friend. Did you know that?" the man stuttered. "You're standing on him like you don't care about his feelings."

"Oh, you mean this windowsill!" the bird exclaimed. "Yes, he's my friend too. It's always nice to take a break from flying now and then, especially considering how high up we are."

"Birds don't talk," the man whispered.

"Oh. Sorry, I didn't know. I just thought it would be nice to have a conversation. I see you looking out this window every day when I fly around," said the bird. The man thought for a moment. Specs of dust drifted past his eyes, suspended in air as if gravity itself had no effect on them.

The man began to feel the mystery sensation in his body. He tapped his finger.

"Okay, what do you want to talk about?" he asked.

"You've been in this room for such a long time," the bird began.

"Yes, weeks," the man interrupted.

"I live life so freely, I can't imagine how you must feel. How does it feel to be trapped? I've never felt what it's like to be trapped," the bird said. The man scoffed.

"Trapped. Hah," he said. He giggled. "I'm the free one." He scanned the bird shuffling on the windowsill. "But you..." the man wagged his finger. "You're a talking bird. That's impossible. Animals can't talk. Not like humans can."

The bird shook its wings. "My associates would have a different opinion," it said. "But please, how do you feel in that cage?"

The man flicked the glass. Startled, the bird jumped back, falling from the ledge. It fluttered its wings and landed back onto the sill with grace. "Cage, what cage, this is my kingdom. I have all the room I need, I have a bed to sleep on, and I'm delivered food. Animal. You have to get your own food," said the man.

"When was the last time you had a breath of fresh air? You know, I could open this window for you, the lock is on my side. Would you like that?" asked the bird.

"No!" the man shouted. "Don't open that damn window."

Cocking its head to the side, the bird blinked its beady eyes. "Come on, just a bit, what's the harm in getting a bit of fresh air?" it asked. The man loosened his tight grip on the sill. He turned his head to the door. His ears twitched. He almost thought he heard the sound of shoes clacking outside. It had been a few weeks. Someone was bound to burst through the door and visit him soon. He looked back to the window to see the bird jumping on the sill. The sun was beautiful outside, the clouds were beautiful. Not like this dark, cold, shallow excuse for a room.

The man's eyes glazed over. A smile curled onto his tired face. "Fine," he said, "open the window." The bird chirped and quickly went to work on the lock, unfastening it with lightning efficiency. A liberating click. The bolt came undone. The man exhaled. With a shaky hand, he reached out towards the window, ready to push it open. Ready to feel the air on his skin.

"Mr. Harvey?" the nurse knocked on the door. Her eyes darted between it, her shoes, and the plastic tray in her skinny hands. The tray carried a single bowl of rice and a single glass of water. "Mr. Harvey, I'm here to give you food. Is that alright? Mr. Harvey?" A shuffle. "Mr. Harvey?"

Mr. Harvey cleared his throat. She heard a feint patter. She refused to exhale should she scare Mr. Harvey away. A moment passed. Then two. She heard a buzzer. A fluorescent red light above the intercom flickered on. Mr. Harvey cleared his throat.

"What is it?" asked Mr. Harvey with a gruff voice. The nurse released the air stored in her lungs. She lowered the tray of food into the slit and saw it vanished to the other side of the door.

"Please eat it, Mr. Harvey, we have a procedure to perform for you in a few hours, it's less painful on a full stomach." A thunderous crash resonated from the door. The nurse jumped back. She heard the plastic tray she had given Mr. Harvey jitter on the ground. A metallic ring echoed through the hall.

"I don't want another one! I'm tired of it!" shouted Mr. Harvey.

"Mr. Harvey, I'm sorry," said the nurse with a crack in her voice.

"Leave me alone!" Yelled Mr. Harvey. The nurse stood still, unsure of what to do. She fumbled with her hand, finally placing it against the door only to remove it a second later. She walked about in a circle, then hurried away.

"A procedure? Is that why they keep you in this cage, Mr. Harvey?" asked the bird. Mr. Harvey kept the bird in his cupped hands, looking at it with tender eyes. Its beak shined brilliantly in the sun. Mr. Harvey, in the dark, simply nodded. "Why don't you come into the sun, Mr. Harvey? Warm your bones." Mr. Harvey, not breaking his gentle gaze with the bird, shook his head. His long, unkempt hair swung at his shoulders. His eyes watered.

"I can't. I might melt. I've been here for weeks," he said.

"But I'm in the sun and you're holding me in your hands. Your hands seem fine to me. Come into the sun," said the bird. Mr. Harvey shook his head once more.

The marching of footsteps echoed outside the door. This time they were more intense. Faster.

"Fly off now," said Mr. Harvey. The bird looked into Mr. Harvey's weary eyes. It gave him a final whistle then took off through the window, leaving Mr. Harvey's hands in the warm embrace of the light.

A knock on the door. "Mr. Harvey, we're coming in, me and the doctors," said the nurse from earlier. A doctor dressed in a flowing white coat hastily swiped a card across a slot beside the door. After a beep and a light, the group of nurses and doctors barged through. They prepared their needles, expecting some kind of resistance.

Mr. Harvey, sitting calmly on his bed, staring at the mess of rice on the floor simply outstretched his right arm. It was littered with small bruises and needle holes, red marks and scratches.

The white mass of coats stalked towards him, a needle at the ready.

"Nurse, close the window," commanded the doctor. "How did he even get it open? I thought the lock was on the other side," he said, flicking the needle tip. Mr. Harvey, limp in the neck, turned to see the sun vanish and the window close, the latch automatically click into place.

"After him we need to go down a floor, to the forty-eighth. There's another one acting up. Rambling about talking animals or whatever."

"Hey," said another. "Be careful with him."

Mr. Harvey felt the jolt of the mystery sensation, looked to his arm, saw the white coat push on the syringe. His eyelids drooped. Mr. Harvey felt the weight of sleep pull him deep into his bed. Another week. Most likely another week.

Mr. Harvey closed his eyes.

A.F. Earnest

The Pharmacist

The door opened and a gust of fresh air pooled into the room. A bell rang with nothing more than a twinkle. Caught by pale moonlight, it glimmered, an extra star in the twilight of the night. Limping, a man emerged from the doorway and made his way towards the desk tucked at the back of the pharmacy. Harsh light from the fluorescent overhead lamps threw his shadow into rows of stacked products between the aisle shelves.

A young woman dressed in a pharmacist's coat was sitting at the wooden desk. She had a freckled face, straight black hair, and deep brown eyes. She glanced up from the mountain of textbooks her face was buried in to see the limping man approaching her. His face was obscured.

"Need any help, sir?" the young woman asked. A few heavy steps later, the man reached the desk. His head was tilted towards the ground and covered by a curved baseball cap.

"What's your name?" asked the man. His voice had a peculiar softness. The young woman closed the topmost textbook from the pile, stood from her chair, and leaned onto the desk with childlike innocence.

"Kyoto," she replied.

"Like the city?" he asked.

"Yeah, like the city," said Kyoto. There was an awkward pause. Kyoto flashed a smile. "Are you looking for anything in particular? Do you have a prescription I can look at?" she asked. The man exhaled and reached into his back pocket. His tie swung like a pendulum, backwards, then forwards. He presented Kyoto with the crumpled piece of paper in his hand. She took the note and briefly struggled to undo the scrunched mess. The note was in a language Kyoto had never seen, with symbols she didn't think existed.

"I'm sorry, I can't read this, Mr...." Kyoto trailed off.

"Tenshi. Naturandzine. I gave all of mine away," said Mr. Tenshi. Kyoto nodded slowly.

"Let me just check to make sure we have some in stock first. Popular thing," said Kyoto. She swivelled to the door behind her back. "Just a minute, please," she said, pushing through the door with her shoulder, her eyes fixed on the prescription in her hand.

Mr. Tenshi leaned forwards. His elbows rested on the wooden desk. The fabric of his shirt was beginning to fade around the elbow area. He took a look around the pharmacy. It was well kept, high-class. There was a healthy tree growing in a plot of soil in the corner. He looked above to see a portrait of Kyoto mounted to the wall, framed with an inscription that gave a brief description about her school internship program. Pretty girl. Pretty name.

"It looks like you're in luck," said Kyoto from behind the door. "As for the price," she continued, now in front of it, "right now a box is two hundred," she finished. Mr. Tenshi sighed. Kyoto was surprised by the amount of air in his lungs.

"That's almost double what I was expecting," said Mr. Tenshi.

"I'm sorry, Mr. Tenshi. It's unfair, but I can't sell it to you for less," said Kyoto. She paused, calculating how to express her sympathy. She placed her hands on the desk and moved closer to Mr. Tenshi, ready to speak. He lifted his head and revealed his face.

His mouth stretched nearly from ear to ear, his teeth were sharp and pointed. His eyes were black, lifeless. Kyoto's pupils dilated. She felt her legs tremble. She darted her gaze over Mr. Tenshi's shoulder and clenched her jaw, trying desperately to stay polite.

"If you still have enough, I can gladly write you up, Mr. Tenshi," Kyoto stammered. Mr. Tenshi focused on her.

"Look at me," said Mr. Tenshi softly. Kyoto's gaze moved to his other shoulder, then to his tie, then fumbled slowly upward to meet his eyes. "It's just how I look, relax, I won't hurt you. You're curious, aren't you?" he asked. Kyoto remained still. "I'm sick. They call it spiritual corruption, whatever that means. I need that medicine," Mr. Tenshi gestured with his head towards the small white box in Kyoto's hands. "Or it gets worse," he said.

"Worse." Kyoto said.

"Worse. I already look like a monster, I know," chuckled Mr. Tenshi. Kyoto gave an airy giggle, although she couldn't tell if it was genuine or nervous. She closed her eyes tightly, composed herself, then opened them.

"Have you been like this your whole life?" asked Kyoto. Mr. Tenshi nodded. Kyoto frowned. She sighed. "How much do you have?" she asked. Mr. Tenshi reached into his pockets and pulled out a wad of bills totalling one hundred and fifty dollars. Clicking her tongue, Kyoto reached into her pocket and got her wallet. She sifted through the bills cradled by the fading leather and counted fifty dollars, leaving her wallet almost empty. She handed the money to Mr. Tenshi, who gave a wide grin in return. Kyoto's eyes widened. Mr. Tenshi handed the bills back to her and Kyoto ran it through the cash register. He took the white box into his hands and gave the lid a caress.

The receipt printed slowly. Each line of text took an eternity to be transferred onto the paper passing through the machine humming away on the desk. Kyoto tapped a finger. Mr. Tenshi simply stared and smiled. The machine beeped. The receipt was done. A silence fell over the shop. The two stood like statues.

"You're aware of all the side effects, how to take the medication? That kind of stuff?" asked Kyoto.

"Yes," said Mr. Tenshi, "Itching eyes, talking animals, muscle weakness. That kind of stuff." Mr. Tenshi ravaged through the box, then at a turtle's pace lifted a single vial from its padding. He brought it up to his black eye. He watched it writhe and twist like thick honey with its own mind. He smiled. "You've been very kind to me," said Mr.

Tenshi. Kyoto gave a shallow bow and a sheepish smile.

"My pleasure," said Kyoto.

"I want to make it up to you," said Mr. Tenshi. He placed the vial carefully into the box. "If you could wish for anything, what would it be?"

"I haven't given it much thought lately to be honest," replied Kyoto. The sprinklers by the tree clicked on. Kyoto and Mr. Tenshi listened to the sound of water being misted into the air and exchanged awkward smiles.

"Don't lie to me. Everyone has something they think about. Something to wish for," said Mr. Tenshi. Kyoto looked to the floor.

"It's not something material," she said.

"So, there is something?" asked Mr. Tenshi. Kyoto nodded. Mr. Tenshi gave a nod then turned away, slowly limping towards the exit. "Consider it done."

The door brushed open. The bell rang. Kyoto lifted her head from the textbook it was resting on. There was a page stuck to her cheek. She brushed it off in a hazy stupor. Kyoto could make out the silhouette of a four-legged animal coming towards her.

"Damnit! How did you even get in here?" she cried, rushing towards the dog. With each new stride, the dog printed a new muddy mark on the floor.

It sat, watching Kyoto intently as she came towards it. Kyoto stopped before the dog. She dropped to her knee.

"You know I have to clean all of this up, right," said Kyoto.

"Sorry," replied the dog. Kyoto blinked. She was speechless. The dog licked its dark coat. "About the mess, that is. I'm here to deliver a message," it said. Kyoto only stared. "Mr. Tenshi would like to remind you that you still have a wish to make," it said. Scoffing, Kyoto crossed her legs and ran her hand through her hair. She wiped her eyes with her palms, dragging them like anchors down her cheeks. "He forgot to mention there's a caveat," said the dog.

"Of course," said Kyoto, rolling her eyes.

"If you helped Mr. Tenshi because you wanted to help, go on and make your wish. If you helped Mr. Tenshi because of some other reason, be careful, your wish might not end up as you expect it to," said the dog. Kyoto pursed her lips. She thought about the night she was having, being careful to remember every detail. She hadn't ingested any of the medication she gave to Mr. Tenshi by accident. She hadn't taken a single drop in her life. She was tired, but she had a good sleep the night before.

The metronomic chirping of crickets outside crept into the pharmacy. Tree leaves rustled as a breeze blew past them. Air flowed through them like water sifting through stones in a river.

"How do I make my wish?" asked Kyoto.

"Are you sure you want to?" replied the dog.

"I don't know," said Kyoto. She stood with a sigh and made her way to the closet where she found a mop and a bucket filled with a soapy solution. "Excuse me, I don't want anyone to slip on the mud you brought in," she said, pointing to the dog.

Each stroke of the mop left a smear of mud and soap that bubbled on the floor. The mop moved in circles, a clockwise motion, retracing covered ground, over and over. It danced in front of Kyoto's unfocused vision. Eventually there was a feint shine of the floor's original cleanliness. Kyoto found herself looking at her reflection.

"That was considerate of you," said the dog. Its tail wagging melodically with the cricket chirps. "Make sure you clean up what I leave on my way out." With a final wag of the tail, the dog slipped through the door. The bell rang for the final time.

Kyoto wiped her forehead with the back of her hand, stopping to listen to the twinkle of the bell. She wondered when she would hear it again. She wondered how long it would take to encounter another person. She looked out the window of her pharmacy, taking in the vast rolling hills and rivers surrounding her in every direction. They were never ending. Kyoto thought about how excited she was for summer to end, how excited she was to go back to the city. Back to school. She was tired of studying ahead for her classes. She was tired of being alone in the pharmacy.

The serene bell faded completely and Kyoto stopped hearing it in her mind's ear. She flashed a glance to the ticking clock on the wall and gripped her mop. It was eleven-eleven in the evening.

A.F. Earnest

The Dreamer

The woman reached into the white box that sat on her bedside table, making sure to be gentle. She grabbed something smooth. A vial. Her hand carried it past her brown hair, past her upturned nose, into the view of her olive eye. The lamp dimmed. A gentle hue of amber trickled onto the wall behind her.

Her other hand, covered in shadow, moved back towards the box. The air was the web her fingers crawled on. She retrieved a slip of paper from the box. She put the vial onto her lap, and brought the paper to her mouth. She licked it. She pinched the paper by the edge and stuck it onto the vial. The paper dissolved into the glass and an ink number appeared moments later. The woman noted the number.

She unscrewed the lid of the vial which could function as a dropper. The fluid inside the vial moved like molasses, slowly swashing against each and every part of its container as though sentient. The woman squeezed the top of the dropper, then loosened her grip. A small dosage of fluid traveled up the glass tube connected to the dropper-lid. The fluid began to glow as she brought the dropper to her mouth. One drop. Only one. That was the number in ink.

Her bed was comfortable. Soft pillows, soft blanket, soft mattress. It engulfed her. She looked to her bedside table, the oak wood made her feel calm. The light went out. The woman lay in the darkness and counted sheep until she fell asleep.

The woman peeled her eyes open as if peeling the skin off of an orange. She sat up. Her mattress felt grainy. It almost felt like she was sleeping on dirt. Some kind of wet forest soil. She jumped up. She was sleeping on wet forest soil.

Frantically, she began wiping wood chips from her cotton pyjamas. After flicking off the last chip from her body, she scanned her surroundings. The comforting amber of her room was replaced by a pale green. The walls were replaced by stretching seas of trees. The still air was replaced with a soft breeze. She wasn't cold.

A whisper slithered into her ear.

"Who's there?" asked the woman. She looked between each tree trunk.

"Say sorry," a voice replied. The woman continued to feverishly comb the trees with her eyes.

"For what?" the woman asked.

"You know what, Danielle," the voice said. Danielle heard a chittering somewhere around her. She looked to her feet. There was a squirrel running around her in circles.

"No, I don't," said Danielle. Having spotted a clearing, she took a step over the squirrel. Her foot landed on a patch of moss. It felt like the softest rug imaginable. She lifted her second leg. The patch of moss buckled under the weight of her foot. A blink. She fell through.

Her foot, now in a casual sneaker, was caught by a red brick road. Danielle was fully clothed. She had her favourite blue coat on. The road was covered by a thin layer of hazy water. Danielle felt as if she was walking on a lake. Up the brick road sat a manor, inviting and innocent. Danielle decided that was where she would go.

"Apologize," said the voice. Danielle hurried her pace. Ripples of water emanated from her feet.

"I don't know you. I don't know what you want. Leave me alone," she said. Her pace turned to a jog. Her steps splashed. She felt her feet getting wet. In between each reverberating splash she heard scratches. Danielle turned her head. The squirrel, with its red coat of fur and beady eyes had followed her. She paid no attention.

"Danielle, just say sorry, it's so easy," said the voice. It was close. Danielle ended her jog abruptly. She turned her head once more. The squirrel stopped too. They gave each other a look. Danielle came to a realization.

"Oh," said Danielle.

"Say sorry," the squirrel said.

"For what?" asked Danielle.

"You know what," it said. It nodded its head towards the manor. Danielle raised her brows. The squirrel gave a blank look. The expression slowly faded from Danielle's face. She cleared her throat and turned to the manor with a pivot on her heel. The manor was steps away. She began to walk.

"I don't know you," she said, moving past the manor gates. Danielle stepped into the yard. Gravel crunched under her shoes. Lamps lined the trail to the door. It was grand. Painted the colour of warm redwood. Danielle shuffled up the doorsteps. She didn't bother to knock. She pushed through the doors and stepped into the manor. Once engulfed in the manor's darkness, the sun and the clouds outside vanished, leaving only pitch black. A light flickered on.

Danielle moved towards the light. As it drew closer, as it grew larger, she found herself without shoes once more. She was in a bathing suit. She was at the beach. She was in the beating warmth of the sun. In the presence of a vast lake. She saw the sand shimmer like glass. It moved at her feet like slow red caramel. So warm.

"You owe it to her. You know that, don't you?" asked the squirrel. Danielle stared at the water, as unmoving and as still as the mountains on the horizon. She spotted her reflection. Her face was a scrambled mess.

"How?" croaked Danielle. "How do I do that now?" she asked. She took a step into the water. It gripped her ankle. The water pulled her in. Waves crashed over her, pulling her deeper and deeper into a hollow abyss. The water pulled with arm-like tendrils, stifling her ability to escape. Danielle screamed. Her voice was dampened by cold water rushing into her throat.

The water spat her out. She found herself completely dry, kneeling in a musty room. The paint was peeling from the walls. The floorboards were damaged, cracked, coming apart. A single bulb dangled from the ceiling.

"Be honest," the squirrel said. Danielle saw two figures at the other end of the room through blurry vision. They didn't notice her. One of them wore a hood. The other looked to be around her height, her weight, her age, wearing her favourite blue coat. The woman took a small white box from the man and gave him a wad of bills in return. The man's smile glistened underneath the hood.

Danielle waved her hand, as if doing so would cause what she was seeing to vanish. Her hand collided with a clear obstruction. Some kind of window.

"Wishing it didn't happen doesn't undo it," said the squirrel. Daniel looked to the animal by her knee.

"It doesn't matter anymore. Seeing it again isn't going to change anything," said Danielle.

"It's not about that," the squirrel said.

"What would you know about it?" asked Danielle.

"Enough," it replied.

"You're wrong," Danielle muttered. She brushed her hair out of the way. Her sight blurred again. She blinked. She was at the beach. Her knees sank into the red sand.

"She's quite pretty," said the squirrel. Danielle shot her head upwards, frantically searching for herself on the other side of the window-boarder. She spotted herself near the water. Her double was standing beside another young woman. Probably her age, maybe a year younger. Blonde hair, blue eyes.

"Please," she turned her head to the squirrel.

"Apologize," said the squirrel. Its voice was cold.

"I'm sorry," said Danielle. Her eyes were red. Itchy.

"Don't apologize to me," said the squirrel. Daniel forced her head back to her double and the young woman. She reached out with her hand, resting it on the obstruction. She saw the two laugh together, talk. It was torturous. Tears began to well in Danielle's eyes. She could hardly see. Everything became obscured by the water beneath her pupils. She shut her eyes.

Danielle opened them. She was in the manor. She was in a room. She saw her double and the girl sitting on a couch, watching something on the television.

"Apologize," the squirrel said. Danielle only opened her mouth. She couldn't muster up any sound. There was nothing she could do but watch. She watched as her double pulled the white box she had traded for earlier out of her pocket. She watched as her double showed it to the girl on the couch beside her, raise her eyebrows and laugh. She watched as the girl said something, then check to make sure they were alone.

"Apologize," the squirrel said. Danielle choked out a whisper. She watched as her double and the girl took a dose from the vial inside the box. Too much. Too big a dose. That was far too much. Too much.

"Apologize."

"I'm—" Danielle began. The carpet at her knees was wet. Filling with water that was rising from the floor. The maroon patterning began to stain. She watched as the two people went limp, their hands gently slip off the couch. She watched knowing one of them wouldn't wake up.

"Apologize."

The forest. The pale light. Danielle stood. Hor-rified.

"Apologize."

"I'm sorry!" she yelled. Her voice echoed through the stilted trees and through the lonely glades.

Her double couldn't hear her cry. It was too busy dragging the slack body of the blonde girl over the forest floor.

Danielle clenched her jaw. She watched as her double threw the girl into a ravine. A thud echoed through the forest. Each echo felt like the scorn of a thousand needles boring further than deep into her heart.

"I'm sorry... I'm so sorry..." Danielle trailed off. The squirrel walked through the window-boarder, leaving Danielle kneeling on the forest floor alone.

Danielle lay still in her bed.

The Detective

"Inspector?" The crunching of dried leaves under a boot filled the air between the trees. "Inspector?" No answer. Muted light coursed through the canopy, bleaching everything in a hazy green. A woman dipped underneath a strand of plastic police tape suspended by the trees it was tied to. She brushed past a figure dressed in a full-body suit and nodded. Spotting who she had been looking for, she stopped just before a man squatting at the bottom of a ravine. She ran a hand through her maroon hair. She gave him a tap on the shoulder. He swivelled his head.

"Oh," he said, "hello, Ms. Olive." He stood from his squat. His knees cracked. "You didn't hear that," said the man. Ms. Olive raised her eyebrows. The detective reached into a pouch on his vest beside his walkie-talkie and retrieved a notebook. He grabbed a pencil wedged behind his ear and scribbled something.

"Who's this?" asked Ms. Olive, pointing skittishly to a body lying in the ravine. The detective, looking rather detached, glanced up from his notebook and turned around.

"Oh, her? That would be Miss..." he paused. The detective flipped through some pages in his notebook, "Miss Mia Summers."

"Is she dead?" asked Ms. Olive.

"Very much so. What are you doing here, Ms. Olive?" asked the detective with a snide smile.

"Mr. Doe," Ms. Olive began, returning a smile of her own.

"Please, call me John," the detective interrupted.

"John," said Ms. Olive, sarcasm dripping from her mouth. "Samantha has been trying to reach you for an hour now." John scratched his beard. His neck became hot. Cursing under his breath, he dashed to his phone. Eleven missed calls.

"Does she still like ice cream?" asked John. Ms. Olive nodded. John turned around. "Timothy!" he called. Another detective on the other side of the ravine lifted his head. He smiled, then waved when he saw Ms. Olive. "I've got to go, it's an emergency, can I trust you to keep our blonde friend company?" asked John.

"Is Ms. Olive a natural blonde? Ms. Olive, hair dye is really bad for you," said Timothy.

"The dead one, Timothy," said John, peeling his gloves off. Timothy looked to the body.

"Ah, right. The autopsy is with Fletcher, John."

"Shall we?" asked John, turning to Ms. Olive. "You can't stay on an active crime scene." He brought his phone to his ear.

Samantha sat in the front passenger seat, seatbelt on, an ice cream cone gripped firmly in her hand. She had a lightly freckled face and a button nose. She couldn't be more than twelve. Her eyes were squinted, battling the sun shining on them. The laces on her cleats were undone. Her jersey had a few grass stains around the hip area. Her expression was blank.

"How was the match?" asked John, looking to his daughter. Samantha sighed and continued to look out the window. John lifted a hand from the wheel and gave Samantha a pat on the shoulder. "I'm sorry, Sammy," he said. A pause. Samantha turned to her father. The radio was off. All was quiet but for the car's spinning tires.

"I didn't score today, just an assist. We lost though," she said.

"Oh yeah?" asked John.

"Yeah. Jen can't aim for shit," said Samantha. Her expression lightened. John smiled. Samantha pressed the button for the radio. The two drove down the tree-lined road.

The house was fairly modern. Open concept. The ceiling in the foyer was slanted. The kitchen and living room were connected. There wasn't much clutter. Samantha sat on a couch, watching television. She gave the striped orange cat on her lap stomach scratches. It purred and wriggled in her hands. There was a glint in its green eyes.

A porcelain bowl clacked as John, focusing on the papers in front of him, tried to fill his spoon with soup. Pictures and reports plastered in ink lay scattered around the table. Pictures of the dead blonde.

John had given up. He took the bowl with both hands and drank from it, not breaking his gaze from the papers.

"How come I can't see?" asked Samantha.

"You'll tell your mom," said John, looking up from the papers. Samantha slid off the couch.

"What if I promise not to?" she asked. John noticed the boredom in her eyes.

"Come here," said John. Samantha scuttled over and stopped just before the edge of the table. She got onto her tiptoes and peered at the picture of the dead blonde. Her eyes didn't so much as widen.

"Where's the blood?" she asked. John lifted an eyebrow.

"There isn't any. We don't think she died that kind of way," said John

"What way?" asked Samantha.

"The blood way," John said. The cat jumped from the couch and ambled to the table, jumping onto it. Its paws kicked away a few papers, revealing a picture of the blonde girl from a closer angle. Her lips were blue, her skin was pale and thinning. Samantha kept a steady gaze. "We think it was an overdose. Not really sure how she got in that ravine though," said John. He reclined in his seat.

"From what?" asked Samantha.

"Medicine," said John. The two exchanged looks. John searched for something in the young pair of eyes across from him. The television blinked behind them. Cosmic colours slathered the walls. Slathered their faces. Samantha looked back at the photograph.

"Medicine is a good thing," said John as he moved his hand over the photo. "Samantha. Medicine is a good thing," he repeated. The pair sat quiet, listening to the television in the background. John ruffled his daughter's hair. He felt a vibration come from his pocket. He fished out his phone and brought it up to his eyes. A text message flashed on the screen. His face sunk. "There's more ice-cream in the freezer, the number for pizza is on the fridge, I hide money in the bowl you gave me last year. I'll be back in a couple hours," he said.

"Yeah," said Samantha. She grabbed the cat from the table and walked back to the couch. John was already headed for the door. He slipped into a coat, took his keys off the key rack, and slipped into some shoes. He checked his coat to make sure he had his badge and opened the door.

"Samantha," John called from outside, "Make sure you take your medicine tonight, okay?"

"Okay," she replied, eyes buried in the television. John nodded and waited a moment until the fresh air cured his disgruntled face. He closed the door.

"Danielle Ardolino? Is that it?" asked Timothy. He gripped his pencil, ready to jot something into his notebook. Danielle nodded. She kept her gaze fixed to the floor at her feet. They were in a small room, lit with warm amber light. The bed was low to the ground. Danielle sat at the edge, the white blanket crumpled around her.

"Do you have any family at home?" asked John. Danielle shook her head. Dark rings lined the bottom of her eyes. She hadn't been getting much sleep. "They know what you're doing?" he asked. Danielle shook her head again. The pair of detectives exchanged looks. It would be a long night.

"Do you have some affairs you'd like to settle? Maybe there's something you do for fun?" Timothy asked warmly. Danielle shook her head. John pointed to the bed, indicating his intention to take a seat. She nodded.

John felt the immediate softness of the mattress and the blanket when he sat.

"Are there any loose ends you need to take care of?" asked John. Danielle scoffed. John continued: "Do you have a favourite spot to eat? A movie you've been meaning to see? Maybe someone you want to get dinner with..." John trailed off. Danielle said nothing. A moment passed. John checked his watch. He put a hand on his knee and prepared to stand.

"You wouldn't understand how it feels," Danielle said under her breath.

"No, I don't think I would," said John gently, staying seated.

"You wouldn't get why we did it," whispered Danielle. Timothy scribbled something in his notebook. John gave him a look. Timothy put his pencil in his pocket. "It's like you're filling the whatever-shaped hole," she said.

"What do you mean?" John asked.

"It's different for everyone," said Danielle.

"Naturandzine?" asked John.

"There's a box in my bathroom. It's the white one. Just take it. I don't want to see it," said Danielle. John was unsure what to do. "Take it. Please," said Danielle. He stood from the bed and walked into the hallway. There were two doors on either side of the hall. John chose the door to his right. "Other door," said Danielle. John opened the door to his left. He was almost blinded by the light bouncing off the tiled floor. Spotting the white box, he made his way towards it, preparing to grab it. His hand stopped just before it.

He thought of Samantha. He didn't want to think about her right now. His hands reluctantly inched closer to the box. He felt his heart palpitate. His hand shook. It was like executing some horrid task. He lashed out and gripped the box, stuffing it into his pocket.

John walked back into the room feeling unnerved. He wanted to go home.

"There'll be investigators over tomorrow to follow up on your story. We need to be going now," said John. He nodded to Timothy who slipped on his coat. "You did the right thing, Danielle," John said. She stared blankly at the floor. "We'll see ourselves out."

The crunching of gravel under car tires. The sun had set. The lights to the driveway flickered on. John stepped out of his car, closed the door and made his way to the house.

He opened the door and stepped into the house to see flickers of light coming from the television, wrapping around Samantha's sleeping body. The cat watched him walk in.

John made his way to the couch, treading lightly, careful not to wake his daughter. On the floor beside her was a white box, just like the one in his pocket. He picked it up, gave Samantha a pat on the head, turned off the television, and went upstairs.

John opened the medicine cabinet. The hinges squeaked. He put Samantha's medicine on a glass shelf. He gently closed the cabinet, afraid that the squeaking would wake his daughter.

He slipped his hand into his pocket to retrieve Danielle's box. He opened the lid and pinched the vial between his fingers. He brought it to his darkened eyes. He watched the clear fluid swirl in the vial for a few minutes. He put the medicine back into the box and put the box on the vanity.

He pushed the medicine out of his mind. He thought about getting a blanket for his daughter.

A.F. Earnest

The Intermission

S potlights covered the floor in light. They flickered, sputtered, buzzed. They died, leaving darkness in their wake. Pink floor lights began to shine through the darkened space. A shoe stepped over one of them, a duffle bag following briefly after.

"What are you gonna do?" asked a timid voice. The shoes stopped. The duffle bag dropped to the ground, stirring up a wave of dust visible only in the pink light. The shoes made their way to the voice: a child curled against a wall. Her hands were wrapped around her knees. Her shield. She was fidgety. Her eyes tracked the tall silhouette approaching her until it froze above her. Her fidgeting stopped. The figure went into a crouch, stifling the floor-light below him. The silhouette's long coat draped over its back.

"What?" asked the stranger. The voice was masculine, confident, maybe even comforting. The girl brought her knees closer to her chest. Her bangs fell into her eyes, obscuring her view of the man's face.

"What are you gonna do?" she asked again. The man made no movement, no attempt at speech. After a moment, he dug into his coat's inner pocket. There was a crisp rustle. His gloved hand presented the girl with a chocolate bar, unopened, with bright yellow wrapping. She brushed the bangs out of her eyes, the grip on her knees loosened. She looked at the chocolate bar, sitting like treasure on the pedestal of the stranger's hand. She glanced up to the stranger's face.

He was wearing a mask. It covered everything except his dark hair. The mask was a blank canvas. A completely white oval, except for the two slit-like eyes, and a semicircle for a mouth painted in black.

"Don't take it," a new voice said from behind the stranger's coat. The stranger twisted his head to see a man huddled against the wall opposite him.

"Are you her dad?" the stranger asked. The man shook his head with fright. "Then shut up and let her do what she wants," he said. He turned back to the girl. Her hands were pressed against the floor, covered by the sleeves of her striped sweater. Cautiously, her hand reached for the bar of chocolate. Contact. No smile. Acknowledgment. She struggled with the wrapper. The stranger gestured with his hand for the chocolate bar. The girl looked between him and the bar of chocolate. The stranger gestured again and she handed him the candy. He made a rip in the wrapper, then handed the bar back to the girl.

The stranger stood from his crouch. He walked through the pink light towards his duffle bag. He grabbed it by the handle, reached into it with his free hand, and fetched a small rectangular device with string wrapped around its back. With the device in his hand, the stranger took several paces to a caged door near the corner of the room. He rattled the cage. A metallic twang echoed. The stranger fastened the device in his hand to the door knob. He took a few steps back.

"What are you waiting for?" another voice asked. The stranger looked to a desk in the corner of the room. It was covered in potted plants, business cards. A feint blue neon tube in the shape of a question mark was bolted on its front. The woman behind the desk had her hands sprawled onto the counter. A metal tag on her shirt caught the shine of the pink floor-light.

There was a small boom on the wall several meters to her left, followed by the sound of twisting metal and concrete rubble dripping onto the floor. A few leaflets danced in the air.

"Come with me," the stranger pointed at her. She exhaled and her leg began to buckle at the knee. "I'll be gone soon, I promise, just come with me," he said. The woman stepped around the desk and walked with raised shoulders towards the stranger. Wasting no time, he took her by the arm and lead her past several frightened people curled against the walls. Some employees, some customers.

The stranger kicked the caged door. The hinges broke from the door frame. Dry wood splintered in a few directions. The door toppled to the floor, letting a rush of cool air carrying a metallic scent blow past the stranger. The white light from the exposed room flooded into the lobby.

"Are you alright?" the stranger asked the woman. She nodded. He stepped into the room. The floor and walls were paneled with wood. The stranger brought her to a cabinet coated in steel, stretching from the ground to the ceiling. There was a keypad next to a lock by the handle. The stranger pointed to the keypad. After a moment of confusion, the woman began to tap some numbers. Darting his head out of the room, the stranger checked to make sure everyone in the lobby was accounted for. They were.

The woman finished tapping in her code, the lock disengaged, the cabinet opened and another rush of cold air blew past the pair. Obnoxiously bright light fell onto the stranger's mask. He stared at the contents of the cabinet. It was almost magnificent, the way those white boxes sat on their shelves.

He reached into the cabinet and pushed row after row of white boxes into his duffle bag. Shelf after shelf, avalanche after avalanche, the stranger's bag filled to the seams with boxes. Leaving the shelves picked clean, he shut the cabinet doors, zipped his bag, and swung it over his shoulder.

He tapped the woman on the arm and pointed his hand to the door. The woman stepped over the fallen door and found herself in the lobby. She stood in the floodlight of the doorway. Her own personal spotlight. Her pupils dilated, she was temporarily blind to the darkness. The stranger's coat brushed past her and slipped into the darkness of the lobby. In strides, he made his way to the exit.

A man leaning against a wall to the stranger's left jumped to his feet. He budged into the stranger's path. The stranger came to a stop.

"Excuse me," said the stranger. The man didn't move. His eyes bore into the stranger's mask. His thinning hair was splotched on his forehead, painted in sweat. His deep breaths were uneven. There was a soft whistle every time he took in air through his nose.

"You know people need those, don't you?" the man asked, pointing a finger to the duffle bag. The stranger took a moment to look at the man opposing him. He drew a gun from his coat pocket. He pointed it at the man's chest.

"Excuse me," the stranger said another time. The man clenched his fists and shook his head. He closed his eyes and whispered something under his breath. "You idiot," said the stranger. He pulled the trigger. The man let out a cry, his hands gripped his chest as he fell onto his knees. The other people in the room were too frightened to make any noise.

Weeping, the balding man searched his chest for an entry wound. There wasn't one. The stranger pulled the trigger again. A stream of water from the gun splashed the man in the face. The water fused with his tears and dripped into his mouth.

The stranger turned around to see the stunned faces behind him. He chuckled, then brushed past the man whimpering on his knees, continuing to the door. He undid the lock to the chain around the handles he had tied earlier. It fell to the floor and jangled. Before leaving, the stranger counted the number of people in the room one more time. He whispered to himself as his finger bounced from person to person. From the duffle bag, he took the same number of white boxes.

"Make these last," said the stranger. He dropped the boxes onto the floor. He reached his hand into the bag one final time, this time grabbing a number of assorted phones. "You can have these back now. Call the police if you'd like," he said. He dropped the phones by the boxes. Lastly, he threw the water gun in his hand to the patch of floor where the girl in the striped sweater was sitting. He pushed through the doors with his back and disappeared into the night. He heard the stampeding of several footsteps and the dialing of several phones.

The moonlight danced in fragments over the lake, cut by the shifting waves. It sprinkled its pale colour over jumping fish. Gulls occasionally made attempts to dive into the water, sometimes coming out with a prize, sometimes empty handed. The stranger drove along a cliffside. Periodically, he glanced past the cliff barricades and sweeping tall-grass to the ocean. In the leather seat beside him, the duffle bag sat still. Buckled in.

The headlights were a strong natural shade of light, venturing on the warmer side of what head-lights could be. They kept track of everything on the dirt road, rocks, holes, the occasional twig. A flat area surrounded by trees overlooking the lake crept into the headlights. The car slowed to a crawl. The engine went quiet. The car came to a stop.

The stranger kept his hands on the wheel. He listened to the breeze, he listened to the singing cicadas, the sound of lapping water. He took in the flashing colours of a Ferris wheel on the lake's pier. He took in the lights from the soaring high-rise covered in vines across the lake. His hands slipped off the wheel. One took the bag by the handle, the other opened the door to the car. He sat a moment longer, lingering, his shoes already outside.

Rocks and dirt scrunched under his feet as he edged closer to the Cliffside. Once he reached the edge of the Cliff, he peered over the barricade. The water was straight below. The stranger unzipped the duffle bag, lifted it with two hands, and tipped it upside down. The white boxes inside scattered to the water below, carried by the wind. They sunk, leaving a string of bubbles.

The stranger reached into his coat to get a small blue notebook and a pen. He undid the clasp and flipped through the pages until he reached a list of various addresses and sketches. Finding the one he had in mind, he crossed out an address.

The stranger looked across the lake to the high-rise. He jotted something down, closed the book, and put it, with the pen, into his coat pocket.

The stranger undid his mask. He held it in his hands. The moonlight made the mask glow in the darkness, its own personal spotlight.

A.F. Earnest

Act Two

A.F. Earnest

The Cat

The sun broke through the window shades and conquered the dark. The room was tinted orange. Metal clanked. A kettle whistled. Porcelain collisions rumbled in space. Drops from a tap fell into a pool of water in a bowl. Someone called. They left through the door. Frantic footsteps dashed down the stairs, past the living room, kitchen, and out the same door. It closed. The key turned in the tumbler. Silence.

After another hour or so, the cat on the couch finally opened its green eyes, trading sun-kissed eyelids for the world. It jumped from its resting spot to the floor, arched its back and yawned. It turned its head to the door. It was shut. The cat sat still for a while, reveling in the peace. Then it flicked its tail and stalked towards the stairs. Catching a glimpse of the first step, it broke into a sprint. An orange streak.

When it arrived at the staircase, the cat spared no time to pause. It jumped onto the steps. Its claws dug into the wood, leaving feint scratch marks as its hind legs propelled it upward. At the top of the steps, the cat made a sharp turn to the left. There was a window at the opposite end of the room facing it. The window was wide open. The cat dashed towards it, jumping over clothes, textbooks, a stuffed rabbit. It sprang upwards and slipped through the window.

The cat momentarily levitated, suspended in the air as if it were a marionette. Then it began to fall. It landed onto a knotted tree branch. The cat's paws absorbed the shock. Some leaves shook loose from the branch. Spotting a patch of grass under the tree, the cat leapt down. It planted its feet on the dewy ground.

The cat continued on its way, not sparing a look to the house behind it. It walked past the gravel drive-way towards the road.

Waves of heat swayed over car hoods and paved brick roads. The traffic was busy, not a minute went by without the honk of a car horn. Men and women, most in black suits, with leather brief-cases, walked about aimlessly. Their polished shoes clacked on the paving. The cat pranced be-tween their legs. None paid attention to the orange bolt navigating below them.

The cat spotted a fountain in a quiet park. The park was surrounded by paving on all sides. It was a small plot of green space, kept in the shade by white trees with red leaves. Some birds splashed in the fountain in the center of the park, lavishing in the small oasis. Delicate little things. Shimmery blue feathers with orange necks. There was a park bench nearby. The cat focused its sight on one bird in particular. The plumper looking one. The cat licked its lips and moved towards the fountain cautiously.

It was over in a second. The cat had jumped to the fountain, claimed its prize by the wing, and landed back on the shaded grass. It dropped the bird at its paws. It squealed.

"Please," the bird said. It felt its fragile heart flutter in its shining chest, "I just wanted water. Just some water for the heat," it said. The cat lowered its head to the ground, so that its slit-like pupils were just across the bird.

"Oh, it's hot, isn't it? Water would be lovely, wouldn't it?" the cat asked. "Do you mind if I have some of your water?" The cat didn't wait for an answer. It jumped to the fountain. The other birds had already flown away. The cat lapped some water down its throat. When it was finished, it landed on the grass by the bird and licked its lips. "Delicious," the cat smiled.

The cat crept closer to the bird, opening its mouth. It lowered its jaw and placed its teeth gently on the bird's skull. Instead of biting, the cat yawned.

"You know, you don't need to be so sadistic about it," said a voice. It was calm, cool, a fountain all its own. The cat's ears perked up. It spotted a man sitting on the bench a few meters away. It hadn't noticed him there before. He was dressed in a dark blue suit, white shirt, no tie. His face was gentle, kind.

"What would you know about it," the cat said, "This is natural, cat-like behaviour."

"Torture is natural?" the man asked. He chuckled. The cat prepared to sink its fangs into the bird's neck. "I heard that bird talk. You heard it too, didn't you? You still wanna kill it?" asked the man.

"As if being able to talk has ever spared lives," the cat said. Annoyed, it readied its fangs once more.

The man stood from the bench and stepped towards the bird. The cat hissed and prepared its claws.

"Shut up," the man said, wafting his hand at the cat. He kneeled, paying no attention to the predator at his feet. He cupped the bird in his hands. It mumbled some thanks. He gave it a smile and put it back in the fountain.

"Idiot, I bit its wing, it'll die in that fountain," the cat said. The man brushed his leg past its orange coat and took a seat at the bench.

"Idiot, it died when you felt like indulging in nature," said the man. The cat looked to the ground.

"Well, it is natural," said the cat. It spoke with a softer tone, maybe with a tint of shame.

"Of course," the man said, "Sadism shouldn't be." The park was tranquil. Not a single car horn could be heard through the thin tree line. Only the swashing water in the fountain made noise.

The suited people walking wherever didn't spare a look. The cat watched them wander. It relaxed its face.

It slowly began to climb onto the bench. Its hind leg slipped. The man put his hand under the cat's dangling paw and pushed it up. The cat took a seat beside the man. They both stared at the suited people shuffling around.

"Do you have a name?" asked the man.

"Whiskers," replied the cat.

"I'm sorry," said the man.

"I'm over it," said Whiskers. Beyond their oasis, amidst the crowd, the two caught sight of a pair of figures arguing. They couldn't hear them, but they could see them waving their hands, clinging onto a white box, engaged in a tug-of-war.

"All this fuss over a tiny white box and a few little drops," said Whiskers. The man arched an eyebrow. He waggled his foot, giving his loafer a shake.

"It's a huge success. Everyone loves filling the hole, don't they," he scoffed. "Do you know anyone taking it?" he asked. One of the fighting figures began to kick the other in the shin. The one being kicked began to scratch at their opponent's face.

"My owner's daughter, actually," Whiskers replied.

"Does she know you talk?" the man asked. Whiskers shook his head.

The man gave his beard a scratch. His face darkened. "You know, it's amazing. What you can actually get away with now. Here we are. Talking animals are a completely normal occurrence as long as it's a side-effect," the man muttered.

"What about you, are you on it? You're talking to me," said Whiskers.

"No," the man replied. He looked ahead.

"And yet we're having this conversation," said Whiskers. He looked over to the fountain to see the bird, leaning against the edge of the fountain bowl. Its breathing was deep, its feathers moved with its breath. "Would you consider me natural?" asked Whiskers.

"I'm undecided," the man replied. The pair continued to watch the combatants from their oasis. The fighters had taken matters to the floor. They grappled and rolled around in the dust, throwing punches and clawing at one another. The passersby simply walked around them, some even turned their heads to see what was unfolding. None actually stopped to help.

The water in the fountain continued to run. A few birds returned. The man and the cat sat in silence and listened to the flowing of the water and the singing of the birds. They might as well have been in a glass box.

"Do you care about her?" asked the man.

"My owner's daughter?" asked Whiskers.

"Yes," the man replied.

"I do," said Whiskers.

"If you care enough you'll find a way to get her off it," the man said. Whiskers spotted two figures emerge from behind the pair sparring on the ground, brandishing batons in their hands. They had white shirts, green arm patches, and walkie-talkies strapped to their belts.

"It does her well, you know. The medicine," Whiskers said. "It's not evil. It's just medicine."

"Yeah," said the man. "Just medicine." He clicked his tongue against the roof of his mouth. He looked over to Whiskers. He smiled. "Get her off of it if you can."

The silence of the oasis was broken by a pair of footsteps. The man turned around and saw two figures come from behind the trees. They looked eager to pull him away from his sanctuary. They were dressed in the same way as the two trying to restrain the people fighting over the white box.

"Ah," said the man. He turned to the cat, "They're for me. It was nice to meet you, Whiskers," the man smiled. Whiskers gave a bow.

"Excuse me Director, would you mind coming with us," a voice said. The man turned over his shoulder and put an elbow on the park bench. He scanned between the faces of those opposing him.

"I thought I told you I was on vacation," said the man.

"I'm afraid it's urgent," said the figure on the left. The man sighed. He put his hand on his thighs and stood up with a stretch. He dusted his suit.

"Fine," he said. They walked past the trees and onto the paving, where they merged into the sea of suits.

Whiskers heard nothing. The birds were gone. The water stopped running in the fountain. Whiskers watched as the two animals on the ground continued to fight over the white box.

The Ferris Wheel

S alty mist was wafted to the pier in spurts, first carried by the water of the lake, then dashed against rock, free to spread wherever it pleased. The sun was gone, leaving only a haze of purple and orange light, a stained, cloudless sky. Seagulls hobbled around, scavenging for crumbs in between moss covered wooden planks. They were careful to avoid the legs stepping around them. They listened to the scattered mumbling of humans infesting the area. They were transfixed by the glowing lights tied to the railing at the edges of the pier.

A Ferris wheel sat at the far end of the pier, quite tall, three or four stories. A couple walked towards it. They were dressed appropriately for the warm weather. Two shorts, two shirts, two low cut shoes, two hands swaying away from each other. They were a comfortable distance apart.

The pair took a sharp left at a snow cone stand, said something to the vendor, paid, then continued on towards the Ferris wheel, guided by the soft lights lining its metallic frame.

Their shuffling came to a slow, then to a stop just before the ticket collector. The two looked above to see the top most carriage, dangling forwards and backwards at the peak.

"What do you think?" asked the first one.

"Yeah, I think that's fine," replied the second. The first one gave two tickets to the ticket collector, who brought a magnifying glass to the tickets. He scratched his neck, clipped the tickets, gave a quizzical look, then handed them back. He pointed to the snow cones. The couple looked at each other.

They finished the cones a few meters away from the line and tossed the scraps into a bin at the foot of the Ferris wheel.

After stepping into their carriage, the two took their seats across from each other. A bar from above fell into their laps and locked into place at their hips. The engine sputtered and the Ferris wheel began its cycle.

The lake to their side moved like a single entity. The waves swayed in unison. It forced their eyes to focus on its existence. It was bordered by mountains. At the end of the lake there was a building standing stories tall, covered in plants and vines. Only the top most light was on.

"So, how are you? How's life?" one of the pair asked, cutting through the silence. His eyes were different shades of the same colour, his hair was messy, his features were soft. "In general. I mean in general," he clarified. The carriage inched closer to the apex of the Ferris wheel.

"I've been fine, just swamped by work. Life's good, Adam. I'm really enjoying it," replied Adam's partner. She giggled.

"That's cool," Adam said. He crossed his arms over his chest, his eyebrows furled. "I heard you got into that program you wanted to, that's great," he said.

"Oh, yeah, I did. Who told you that?" A polite chuckle. The Ferris wheel creaked as it was pushed by the breeze. Their carriage rocked softly back and forth.

"Just one of your friends," Adam said, "Dani."

"Oh, yeah, I got in," a forced laugh, "It's cool that you're still hanging out with her."

Adam gave a polite smile. His teeth were tinted blue from his snow cone. A moment later he realized that his teeth might be stained, so he closed his lips. He made a mental note not to show too much tooth from this point.

"Yeah, we're pretty close. I wouldn't have heard about it if it wasn't for her," Adam chuckled. He wrapped his hands around the safety bar. They were starting to sweat.

He had rehearsed this conversation in his head countless times, never expecting it to actually be spoken. He thought about all the potential things he would say a hundred, no, a thousand times over.

"I'm sorry," the hand across from him reached over and gently touched him. "I was planning to tell you, I was just so busy with work."

"Yeah, it's cool, I get it," Adam smiled. He closed his lips. The conversation was going right where he thought it would. It went here seven times out of ten. The Ferris wheel was nearing the apex. The air started getting cooler. Some stars began to shimmer in the purple bits of the sky.

"I miss talking to you."

"Don't say that," Adam said maybe too quickly. His eyes darted to the comfort of the lake. "Don't say that," he muttered. "Don't say that if you don't mean it," he said. The hand withdrew.

"Of course I mean it, Adam, you're my best friend."

"Are you kidding me?" Adam asked. He froze. He had never thought about what to say past this point. The conversation never played out further than this in his mind. "How long has it been since we last hung out?" he asked.

"Come on, that's not fair, you know how busy I am."

"You're not that busy," Adam scoffed. There was a pause. "Over a year, if you're wondering," he said.

"I meant it, you're one of my closest friends."

"Just stop saying that," Adam said. He felt his voice get tense. "Don't you understand what you're doing to people? You can't just throw those words around like they don't mean anything," he said. He ran his hand through his hair. It fell back onto his forehand in strands. He took a deep breath and regained his composure. "I get it. We're not what we used to be. Why are you making it so hard for me to accept that?" he asked.

The two sat in silence. The Ferris wheel let out creaks and groans synonymous with rusted metal. Adam cupped his face with his hands. The Ferris wheel clicked into place at the apex and hushed.

It was as if everything else in the world stood still, even the lake below them. Adam reclined into his seat, his breathing was deep. He calmed himself.

"I don't know what else to say," he said. He slipped a hand into his pocket and gripped a square shaped box. He ran his thumb longingly over the lid, back and forth.

"Adam, I understand how you feel. I mean that. I'm sorry. I've just been really busy."

"Come on," Adam said. His eyes stared ahead. "We go months at a time without talking. I know what it's like to be busy," he said. A white box came out of his pocket. He pressed it against his lap. "You don't understand what you do to people," he said. Adam stared at the white box on his knee. It was more interesting than the view to the lake, or the person in front of him.

The light in the topmost floor of the high-rise at the end of the lake went out. It was dark. Whatever orange was left in sky after the sun had set was gone, overpowered by violet. A sliver of blackness squeezed past the mountains. The stars became brighter.

Adam looked up from his knee to the girl sitting in front of him. She was smiling. Her teeth were glowing with an almost unnatural whiteness.

Red soaked the cracks between her teeth, the rem-
nants of a snow cone.

Adam bit his lip. Without thinking, he threw
the small white box into the lake. It landed with a
small splash, began to sink, then was gone. Some
bubbles popped on the surface where it had disappeared.

"Litterbug." A strained giggle.

Adam looked at the seat across from him. His
face was relaxed, cold, without emotion.

The girl was gone. The Ferris wheel began to
creak and groan once more. The engine sputtered
and continued to hum with indifference. A statue,
Adam stayed frozen while the carriage began its
descent. A metal rod had replaced his spine. His
eyes were locked to the front, to the seat on the
other side of the carriage.

At the bottom of the Ferris wheel, the metal bar
at Adam's hip clacked. He pushed it over his shoulders. Adam sat for a moment before swiveling out
of his seat. He wiped his sweaty palms on his
shorts. The darkness of the night had set in. The
stars were out. The pier was empty. Adam turned

his head. He took a step away from the Ferris wheel.

"Hey," a gruff voice said from behind. Adam stopped dead in his tracks. "I saw you throw something from the top of the wheel. What was that?" It was the ticket collector. Adam turned his head a quarter twist. He saw him approaching in the periphery of his eye.

"I don't know," Adam shrugged. The ticket collector shook his head and turned away. Adam began to walk down the pier.

He walked in the middle of the pier. There was not another soul in sight. He found the flashing lights on the railing comforting. Soothing. He felt his phone vibrate in his pocket. Another time. He took the phone out of his pocket and pressed it to his ear.

"Hello?" he asked. "Hello?" he asked again.

"Hey, Adam!" the voice on the line laughed, "What are you up to right now?"

"Not much," Adam said, reaching the end of the pier. He stopped at a wooden staircase draped in moss. It led to the beach. "I was just at the pier. What about you?" he asked. He stepped onto the staircase. It rasped.

"I just got off work," the voice chuckled, "I was wondering if you wanted to do something this weekend? It's been a while!" the voice continued. Adam continued down the steps without hurry, drawn to the waves rolling onto the sand.

"Yeah, sure, let's do it," he said absentmindedly.

"Okay, great, we'll work out the details a bit later then!"

"Yeah, sure, whatever you say," Adam finished. He ended the call and slipped his phone into his pocket. He stepped onto the beach. His shoes sunk into the sandy curves.

The lake was moving how it had always moved. Adam took his shoes off and left them on a nearby rock near a support pole for the pier. The warm, white water was inviting.

The Director

L eather squeaked. A suit rustled. The low rumble of an engine, freshly cleaned, hummed and droned. It was like a humming bird. The driver listened to the nectar at his ears. The car was new, taken care of, remarkably spacious in the back. The Director sat with his legs outstretched, reading the day's newspaper, holding a glass of water. The two figures that had collected him from his oasis earlier sat at his sides.

"Director, do you need time to prepare anything?" asked a voice. It was soft.

"Who's asking?" the Director replied, turning to the woman who asked the question.

"Mr. Stevens," she replied. The Director rolled his eyes and turned away. The car passed over a bump in the road. It went unnoticed. Mostly. The driver turned around. The Director waved his hand to shoo him away.

"He'll know when I get there," said the Director. He took a sip of water.

"Director, do I have to work this weekend?" asked the woman.

"Who's asking?" asked the Director.

"My daughter," replied the woman. The Director turned to her and gave a wink.

"No, Ms. Olive, there's no need for you to be working on the weekend," he said. Ms. Olive gave a nod and a smile. She scratched at the green band around her arm.

"Thank you, Director," she said. The car slowed to a crawl. The road felt like butter.

Having rolled the windows down, the Director felt a breeze flow through his hair. He reached into his suit pocket for a pair of sunglasses, unfolded them, then put them on. The car came to a stop. Ms. Olive exited first and held the door open for the Director.

She closed the door behind him, taking care not to trap his suit in the car. The Director bent his head back. He was looking directly above, taking in the view of the high-rise towering above him. Its walls were plastered in vines, trees, delicate flowers, and dark splotches of moss growing on the glass and concrete.

"Is Mr. Stevens on the ground floor?" asked the Director, lowering his head and massaging his neck.

"The top floor," Ms. Olive replied.

The elevator was smooth, not a jitter to the left or the right. A number dashed across a screen on the elevator door for each floor passed. The Director's sunglasses were hanging from his suit pocket. Only Ms. Olive was at the Director's side. She was on her phone, scrolling through a body of text. Some pictures of a bright room with the door blown off were spliced between the paragraphs.

The elevator gave an electronic ring. The door opened with a feint, high pitched whir. The upper-most floor was barren. There was a couch facing a large window. It overlooked a mountain range and a lake. An office was hidden in the corner. It was plastered in various film posters and newspapers. The blinds were down and the door was shut.

The two stepped out of the elevator and onto the tiled floor. It was spotless. The Director worried about tracking in some dirt from his shoes.

A man was waiting for them, middle aged, in shape, silver hair, he wore a bright dress shirt.

"Ah Director, thank you for coming, how was your vacation?" the man asked, making his way towards the pair.

"I would hardly call it that, Mr. Stevens. What am I here for?"

"Mr. Tenshi is waiting for you in your office, Director," said Mr. Stevens.

"Is he?" the Director raised his eyebrows. "Ms. Olive, take the day off, I don't want to see you until after the weekend," he said. Ms. Olive flashed a smile and stepped into the elevator. The door closed behind her, leaving the Director alone with Mr. Stevens. He chewed on a stick gum. The noise it made did a good job filling the emptiness of the floor. "Shall we?" the Director asked with a gesture towards the office.

The desk had a few leaflets scattered on it, some papers in a stack, a printer. Isolated on the other side of the desk, there was a tiny tree growing in a clay pot.

The Director sat reclined, his back turned to a wall of glass overlooking the mountain range and the lake. Leaning against the office door, Mr. Stevens continued to chew his gum. The Director gave him a look and pointed to a bin in the corner of the office. Mr. Stevens took the gum out of his mouth and flicked it into the bin.

The Director looked at the person sitting in the chair across from him. He was dressed in a bright windbreaker. He had a baseball cap and a surgical mask. He looked back with beady black eyes, empty of life, emotion. Anything.

"You've done well for yourself," said Mr. Tenshi.

"And you're still in the chair in front of me, Mr. Tenshi. That time of the year again? Come for another culling?" the Director asked.

"I prefer to call it a contract," said Mr. Tenshi. He lowered his surgical mask, revealing his toothy grin below. The Director swivelled in his chair, turning to the window behind him. A bird flew past, then spotting some food below, began to dive.

"Not interested in asking me how I've been?" asked the Director. He darted his gaze between the mountains and the lake. The sun danced on the waves.

"How have you been?" asked Mr. Tenshi.

"I was just on vacation, actually," said the Director. He kept his steady gaze on the twinkling lake.

"How was that?" asked Mr. Tenshi.

"You ruined it," the Director said with a smile. He turned back to Mr. Tenshi. "Mr. Stevens, leave the room, please," the Director said. Mr. Stevens turned around, opened the door, and left the room, closing the door behind him. There was a brief moment of silence, followed by the whirring of the elevator. Mr. Tenshi smiled.

"One hundred," said the Director.

"No," said Mr. Tenshi. "We had a deal. Don't lowball me."

"I don't care, I'm tired of this," said the Director. Mr. Tenshi stood from his chair and gave a chuckle that made the hair on the Director's neck stand as if possessed.

"But Mr. Director," Mr. Tenshi mocked with a childish tone, "What about sacrifice?" he asked. He skulked over to the Director. He gripped him by the shoulder and forcefully turned him towards the window. "Eleven hundred and eleven," said Mr. Tenshi.

"No," said the Director.

"Mr. Director," Mr. Tenshi said. His voice soured. A clicking noise came from the back of his throat. He licked his teeth. "I would have assumed you would stick to your word," said Mr. Tenshi. "Partner." Like brushing off a leaf, the Director flicked Mr. Tenshi from his shoulder.

"I don't remember putting that on paper," said the Director. He paused, focused on the lake outside. It was beautiful. It had always seemed beautiful to him, but especially so in this moment. The moment passed.

The Director cleared his throat. "To Hell with it. I'm ready."

"Oh," said Mr. Tenshi. He laughed. "You really are a man of sacrifice."

"What do you say?" asked the Director. There was a pause.

The Director reached into his pocket and grabbed something. He stepped forwards. He raised his stretched arm and used the window as a backdrop to view what he was holding. It was a butterfly carved from maple.

He took a moment to admire it. The craftsman-ship was terrible. It might as well have been made by a child. The Director put it onto his desk next to the tree. "What do you say to mine?" he asked. Mr. Tenshi grinned.

"I think that sounds lovely," said Mr. Tenshi. He reached for the butterfly on the desk.

"Don't touch that," snapped the Director. Mr. Tenshi's hand stopped dead in its track.

"Hit a soft spot, have we Mr. Director?" Mr. Tenshi asked. His hand changed its course for the tree. He grabbed the pot and brought it to his chest. Extending a finger, he made contact with one of the leaves. The tree began to wither and twist. It turned black and evaporated into ash. It gave off the noise of wood crackling under the heat of a fire.

"And I can trust you to keep your word, Mr. Tenshi?" asked the Director, focusing on the wooden butterfly. Mr. Tenshi almost looked offended.

"Of course, Mr. Director. I'll even put it on paper," he said, holding the empty pot in his hand. He touched the soil. A new tree began to grow, this one with leaves of deeper colours and branches with interesting twists and loops. There were other-worldly symbols etched around the plant's body. "I'm not a monster." Mr. Tenshi set the pot with the new tree back onto the table next to the wooden butterfly. The Director gave Mr. Tenshi a nod.

"And you know what to do?" asked the Director.

"I know what to do," replied Mr. Tenshi. The two exchanged a look. "Do you regret this? Our little venture," he asked. The Director turned to the window. "Do what you said you'd do," said the Director. He crossed his arms. Mr. Tenshi stepped beside him.

"It's a lovely view," said Mr. Tenshi. He was genuine. "You've helped a lot of people, Harvey. I don't know many people who'd go as far as you did." He gave him a pat on the shoulder. "I wish I hadn't given you an offer you couldn't refuse," he said. Harvey turned to face Mr. Tenshi. The two shook hands.

"I regret it," said Harvey. Mr. Tenshi nodded with understanding.

"It won't take anyone anymore, Harvey. Your sacrifice is appreciated. I can return the people taken in the last week. I'm keeping the rest for myself. Consider it a parting gift," said Mr. Tenshi.

"Thank you," said Harvey. "Whenever you're ready," he said. Mr. Tenshi smiled. He touched the sprawling window at their side. It vanished. A breeze came into the room. It scattered papers. Caught by the wind, some flew outside. Harvey gave a nod. Mr. Tenshi gave him a push. Harvey fell to the lake below. Mr. Tenshi touched the spot where the window was. A new one appeared in its place. A butterfly flew across his back.

A.F. Earnest

The Grave Digger

C ascades of dirt fell. Each grain contributed to the ocean of earth at the tree's base. A shovel stabbed at the ground. A boot kicked it further in. A pair of hands twisted the handle, amassed a sizable amount of dirt on the blade, and threw it to the side.

The sun was blocked by dark clouds. A marble on the blanket of the sky. Neither blue nor black, just existing, listening to the rhythm of the digging.

Surrounded by piles of earth, tall and tanned, his shirt dangling from the back pocket of his faded jeans, stood the man working the shovel. His back was broad, his shoulders were wide, his brow was wet with his labour. After one final stroke, the man dropped the shovel to the ground. He stood still, looking at the hole he had dug. He clawed at the patch of mud on his cheek.

The hole was in the shape of a rectangle, not perfect, but large enough to work. The man looked to the casket on his right and lifted his hand. His thumb jutted out from the rest of his grouped fingers at a ninety-degree angle. He lined up the angle with the bottom right corner of the casket, squinted, then being careful to preserve the shape of his hand, lined it up with the hole below him. It would work.

He moved behind the casket and clapped his hands. He bent over and began to push. It was light, light enough to push at least. The lifting machine had broken over the weekend much to the gravedigger's dismay. The earth tore away in strips at his boots as he pushed on the casket with extended arms. After a brief struggle, it fell into the hole. The man exhaled. He took a seat at the edge of the hole, letting his legs rest on the casket. He wasn't squeamish.

A thump.

The man looked behind his back, expecting to see someone bobbing between the gravestones and trees. There wasn't anyone. Another thump. This time he felt his feet move. Another thump. The casket below him began to shake, shedding stray dirt like a dog shaking water from its coat. The grave digger recoiled with a jolt of energy. More thumping, each new thud from the casket became louder and more intense. Finally, the lid burst open.

A woman, her skin intact, maybe a bit pale, dressed in a white gown gasped for a breath of air. The gravedigger, eyes wide, kneeled at the edge of the hole.

"Hey," his voice cracked, "Let's get you out of there." The woman grabbed his hand and he pulled her out of her grave. After crawling out of the hole, she leaned against the tree, taking huge breaths at a speed that truly astounded the grave digger. She flailed her hands, as if desperately longing to hit something. She settled on tearing her gown. It became a skirt. The gravedigger didn't know what to say.

"Ma'am, are you alright?" he asked, unsure what else to add. A crow landed on a gravestone nearby and cawed. The woman looked at the gravedigger with clouded green eyes. "Ma'am?" he asked again.

"You've got to put me back," said the woman. Her eyes darted to the casket she was in moments ago. As if transfixed, she took a step towards the hole. The gravedigger gripped her cold wrist, keeping her dangling like a doll before pulling her back. He propped her against the tree.

"Wait, hold on, what are you talking about, you're still alive!" he exclaimed. The crow took flight from the gravestone and landed on the gravedigger's shoulder. Its nails dug into him. They scratched him.

"No, she's not," said the crow. The gravedigger looked to his shoulder. He looked back at the girl. Her attire was grimy, smeared in dirt, her muddy eyes looked distant.

"It's true," she said, "It's over for me. I think I just want to be in my casket now," she said. She pushed herself from the tree, and with a bare foot, took a step past the gravedigger. She jumped into the hole before dusting away at the dirt caking the satin inside the casket. The gravedigger watched her clean her grave in a state of disillusion. He looked again to the crow on his shoulder.

"You think I should let her go through with this?" he asked.

"Just another body," it replied. The woman, now in her half-tidy casket reached to the lid and gripped it with her spindly fingers.

"You'll bury me, won't you?" she asked with a smile. The gravedigger paused, contemplating the implications of his decision, regardless of what the crow told him, he still felt an uneasy rolling in the pit of his stomach. He felt a certain restlessness, a disquiet. The punch of an opportunity.

"What did you see," he asked, ignoring her.

"What?" she asked.

"When you died, what did you see?" the gravedigger asked. The woman smiled.

"The most beautiful thing. It was so clear. So warm. Flowing like sweet molasses. It was glowing. I felt like I had everything I wanted and everything I didn't know I wanted," she explained. The gravedigger paused. He reflected on what the woman told him. He pursed his lips and looked to his shovel, then back to the woman.

He reached for the shovel with his callused hand. The crow flew from his shoulder and landed on a gravestone. One of its feathers came undone and descended into the casket. The woman struggled to fit the lid of the casket into place, but finally managed. The gravedigger was left standing atop the earth overlooking the hole. He gripped the shovel.

Borrowing earth from the mountain of dirt to his side, he found his rhythm once more and began filling the hole. As the gravedigger continued to shovel and the mountain continued to shrink, he felt like he could hear the faintest of thumps at his feet. He chose to ignore it. He was engrossed in his rhythm, obeying the feelings in the pit of his stomach. He began to hum, drowning out the thumping below.

The crow landed on his shoulder again. He continued to dig.

"Do you believe her?" it asked.

"Maybe. Best not to think about it now," the gravedigger said. "I'm just filling the hole."

The gravedigger patted down the remaining soil on the plot. The mountain at his side was gone, the earth at his feet was dark and wet. The thumping was weak, slowing down, fading from his memory. He moved to the tree where the dirt mountain once stood and sat down. He put his aching back against the firm trunk. The crow sat in a branch above him. The sky was still hazy. Still grey. The clouds didn't move. The gravedigger looked to the spot where the casket once was. He stretched his neck.

"You've still got another one to go today," said the crow. The gravedigger looked to his left. Another casket. This one was made from a more expensive material. The brass clasp was done firmly.

The edges were lined with ivory. A bouquet of white flowers was placed in a basket bolted to the lid of the coffin. The gravedigger sighed and kicked at the air with his boot.

He ran his hand across the grass beside him, then reached into his pocket. He dug until he fetched a small white box. He reached into the box to get a vial. He undid the lid and measured a dose. With a glass dropper, he placed a dosage of the clear, molasses-like liquid onto his tongue. His pupils dilated then shrank. The gravedigger put the vial back into the box and put the box back into his pocket. He stood from the tree, his hand outstretched, anticipating the cold grip of the shovel.

A thump. This one was louder, closer. The gravedigger looked to the casket with the ebony trim. It was still. A thump. The casket moved. The gravedigger ran over and quickly began to undo the clasp with manic hands. The crow began to caw. He fumbled with the metal clasp, finally managing to lift the lid of the casket, but cutting himself in the process. He flicked some blood onto the flowers. Upon seeing the contents of the casket his manic demeanour ceased. His hand slipped away from the lid, leaving a bloody mark. He smiled.

"Hi," he said with a certain confidence. The woman inside darted her head to the left, to the right, back to the left. Her blonde hair waved like prairie grass. Her blue eyes rolled in their sockets, eager to make sense of the situation they found themselves in. She opened her mouth as if to speak, but no words came out. Only gasps and chokes.

"Do you know who you are?" the gravedigger asked. The woman turned her jittering head to face him, her eyes continued to roll aimlessly in any direction they thought to roll in.

"Summers," she stammered. The gravedigger reached into his pocket for the white box. He quickly undid the lid, measured a dosage, and brought the vial to the woman. She slapped his hand as it approached. The grave digger recoiled in surprise. He put the vial back into the box and tucked the box into his pocket.

"What did you see. When you died?" he asked, his eyes lighting up like lanterns. There was a rhythmic thumping from the casket in the soil. The crow cawed.

"Nothing." The woman croaked. The grave-digger's lips curled into a smile. He stood from his knee and grabbed his shovel. He towered over the woman in the casket. He felt the digging rhythm beat in his heart. He began to tap his foot to the thumping coming from underground.

"Just another body," said the crow. The smile faded from the grave digger's face. He sat down and propped himself against the tree.

The End

"A water gun?" he asked. He gave a dry chuckle. A seat buckle came undone with a satisfying click. Another one shortly after. Two door handles were pulled, and two car doors opened. Two pairs of shoes crunched onto the gravel road. The man on the left side of the car closed his door first. The car gave a short beep. The man on the right side of the car turned to face the man on the left side. Their eyes met over the roof.

Each face was partially distorted by the dancing waves of heat jumping from the car top. Their eyes were squinted to shield themselves from the glare of the sun overhead.

"I don't want to kill anyone, John, just help them," said the man on the right. He brought his hand to his face to act as a visor.

"You rob people, Benjamin," said John. He walked to the front of the car. Benjamin met the man at the front of the car where they stood a foot length apart from one another. "One more time, Benjamin, and I'll do something about it," said John.

Pine needles rustled. A cliff barricade rattled in the breeze. The lake glistened. The pier was busy with people going about their day, buying food, sitting under coloured umbrellas on coffee shop patios. The high-rise at the end of the lake stood as it always had. It was imposing, dominating, yet the plants coiled around its walls made it feel welcome in the skyline. It was both so repelling and tantalizing. It was pervasive.

"Of course, Detective Doe," Benjamin said. He gave a smile. John clicked his tongue.

"Stop it, Benji," said the detective, stifling a laugh. Benjamin just stood still, his eyes burning in the light. He lowered his hand visor and turned his back to John.

"What do you say we find a spot in the shade?" he asked.

The pair sat atop a wooden picnic table under the shade of a tall pine tree near the edge of the cliff. They had the park to themselves. It was empty, save a few birds chirping somewhere. The wind seemed to settle. Heatwaves continued to rise into the air from the earth. Anything they passed through became mirage-like. Benjamin passed John a bottle of water. He took a few big gulps. Some rogue drops slid down his chin and fell onto the dirt below him, stirring up a cloud of dust. John wiped his chin.

"I'm having a barbeque tonight, what does your schedule look like?" he asked.

"I had some plans this evening," said Benjamin.

"It's gonna go late into the night, you're welcome to stop by," said John.

"I'll give you a ring," said Benjamin, taking the phone out of his pocket. He gave it a shake. "How does that sound?" he asked. John handed the bottle of water back to Benjamin, who took a drink for himself.

"Sammy will be happy to see you," John said. Benjamin nodded with the bottle in his mouth. He watched it drain as cool water slipped down his throat. "Make sure you bring your niece a present."

The sun had set and left a trail of thin clouds suspended in the mellow sky. The last rays of the day's heat had vanished from the earth, the roads, the waters until everything was finally still. A cool wind came with the night.

Little by little, various windows began to shine with white light. For each house Benjamin drove past, a new light flicked on. The horizon facing him was pink and orange. The road behind him was smeared white on account of the street lamps. They turned on after he drove past them.

He continued to drive until the high-rise with the plants growing on its walls came into sight. Only the bottom and top floor had their lights on. The rest of the windows were darkened, tinted orange by the sky. Benjamin found a place to park on the street across the building.

He shut the engine off and sat in his dim car for a moment. The street lights had caught up with him. The car bathed in white light.

Benjamin opened the glove compartment and his mask tumbled onto the duffle bag on the seat beside him. He took it in his hands, brushed it, gave the slit-like eyes a look, then fastened it to his face. Benjamin rummaged through the duffle bag, and after finding what he wanted, slipped something into his coat pocket.

He stepped out of the car, closing the door behind him. He walked onto the desolate street and paced towards the high-rise.

A raccoon from a nearby trash bin ran into his path. "Are you sure you wanna do this?" the raccoon asked. Benjamin stepped over it, not breaking his stride.

"I'm sure," said Benjamin. The doors opened automatically when Benjamin stepped onto the welcoming matt.

He went through and found himself in the lobby. His foot landed on a soft rug. It was velvet, a deep burgundy colour. Trees grew in plots by the corners of the expansive area. There was a garden in the center of the lobby, with flowers and plants of all kinds. The edges were lined with more trees.

Benjamin spotted the welcome desk. There was no one behind it. There was no one around.

His shoes clacked on the floor as he made his way to the desk. He vaulted himself over to the other side. Benjamin began to rummage through drawers and ruffle papers. The sound of crumpling pages echoed through the lobby. There was a pause. The final few sounds stifled themselves out. Benjamin found what he was looking for. He spread a sheet of paper out on the desk, then traced a finger around the ink.

He made his way to the elevator, dropping the sheet of paper behind him.

The elevator dinged, the doors slid open and revealed a couch facing a window overlooking a lake and a mountain range. There wasn't much else on this floor. Benjamin stepped out of the elevator and heard the doors close behind him. Silence. The stillness made him uneasy. He couldn't help himself. "Hello," Benjamin called out. Not even a whisper.

Benjamin took a cautious step to the window. His coat brushed by the couch. The sight of the lake and the mountains was inspiring.

He slowly rotated his head, struggling to remove his gaze from the scenery. He saw the office on his side. He liked how it looked. It looked natural. Like it belonged to a human. He felt comforted by the film posters and newspapers taped to the walls.

Benjamin gave a knock on the door. No reply. He turned the door handle. The door opened itself. The room had no one in it. There was an interesting plant on a desk, with bizarre symbols etched into it, and a butterfly carved out of wood beside it. Papers were scattered on the floor. Benjamin turned out of the office and gently closed the door behind his back.

His eyes moved from the floor to the wall. A flickering white light coming from around the corner caught his attention. Benjamin found himself drawn towards the light. It grew brighter. It grew clearer. Benjamin turned the corner. His silhouette was struck by light. There was no room for shadows here.

Benjamin stopped dead in his tracks. His arms went slack and dropped to his side. His mask covered his gaping jaw.

Benjamin stood in front of a glass cylinder. It stood meters tall, a few meters in diameter. Vines with budding flowers were wrapped around the glass. The vessel almost would have looked empty if it weren't for the occasional bubble of air that sloshed up and down. The fluid inside looked as if it was moving by itself, without any influence. It was unpredictable, spontaneous movement, like the twisting of waves in an ocean. Benjamin found himself stepping closer to the glowing liquid.

Slowly, he drew the rectangular device he had taken from his duffle bag out of his pocket. His breathing deepened. He stared at the explosive in his hand. He continued his approach towards the massive container. His hand reached towards his mask. He undid the clasp in the back. The mask fell to the floor. The vines around the container constricted. Benjamin squinted. His heart began to race. His mouth felt dry. He hadn't blinked since he entered the room.

Benjamin was at the glass vessel, his head only centimeters away. He looked again to the bomb in his palm. He lifted his free hand and pressed it against the container. He felt it move, heard it hum. He felt a connection. He felt as if all his problems were taken care of. Now, and forever to come. He felt understood. Validated. Fresh. He felt his chest lighten, loosen, relax.

Everything would be fine. Nothing mattered. There were no issues that needed thought or attention. They were thought of. There was nothing to be afraid of. Fear didn't exist. There was no need to think about fear. Thinking didn't exist. Nothing mattered. Everything would be fine.

Benjamin's eyes were fixed on the road. His mask was on the seat beside him, nestled on top of his duffle bag. His hands were loose on the steering wheel. His phone was tucked into a cup tray by the hand break. He checked the hour on the dashboard. He thought he would have enough time to stop by his brother's barbeque. His eyes scanned the sides of the road for any convenience store or gas station. He figured he would need to get Samantha something. He couldn't help but smile.

A.F. Earnest

Acknowledgements

A special thank you is extended to anyone who participated in the completion of this project in any way. Thank you, Max, John, Mady, Tim, and Ed, for being kind enough to look over the earliest versions of the manuscript, to offer your initial thoughts, impressions, and critiques. Thanks again, Mady, for accepting to do the cover art. A thank you to my parents, for their support of my creative endeavours, their warmth and compassion, and for their input and feedback on this project.

To anyone who has enjoyed and supported any of my content in the past, in any form or medium, through viewership, or financially, thank you. Your continued feedback and support has helped me improve, and has been a source of great inspiration.

Last, but certainly not least, thank you, reader. All the best to you.

Until next time,

A.F. Earnest

A.F. Earnest

About the Author:

This is A.F. Earnest's first official publication, though he's dabbled in storytelling before. He wants to assure you that all his previous work is really quite prestigious. However, this is his first official author bio. He hopes he's doing a good job. He doesn't really know, it's a bit hard to tell without any feedback or guidance. You'll go easy on him, won't you? He hopes to retire at an early age to a secluded woodland village, where he can continue telling stories, and raise a flock of sheep.

Nice

87057883R00074

Made in the USA
Columbia, SC
10 January 2018